Bobby,
Charlton and
the Mountain

11

Praise for
Bobby, Charlton and the Mountain

'An outstanding début novel,
warm-hearted, moving and memorable.'
The Bookseller

'An excellent story . . . the first-person voice
of the narrator is so immediate, so animated.'
T.E.S.

'A heart-warming story about sibling solidarity.'
The Teacher

Bobby, Charlton and the Mountain

SOPHIE SMILEY

Illustrated by

MICHAEL FOREMAN

Andersen Press • London

First published in 2003 by
Andersen Press Limited,
20 Vauxhall Bridge Road, London SW1V 2SA
www.andersenpress.co.uk
Reprinted 2005, 2007, 2008

British Library Cataloguing in Publication Data
available
ISBN 978 1 84270 178 2

Mixed Sources
Product group from well-managed
forests and other controlled sources
www.fsc.org   Cert no. TT-COC-002227
© 1996 Forest Stewardship Council
FSC

Phototypeset by Intype London Ltd
Printed and bound in Great Britain by
CPI Bookmarque Ltd, Croydon, Surrey

For Thomas, William and Piete

Chapter 1

My family is football mad! Mum and Dad are so football crazy they even spent their wedding day at a football match.

Dad asked Mum: 'How many kids do you want?'

And she said, 'A whole football team!'

When they got to me he said, 'Well, we've made it to five-a-side!'

I was born with loads of ginger hair, and Dad started singing, 'Come on, you reds!' He was embarrassing even then!

It was Dad's idea to call me Charlton, but everyone calls me Charlie. At school they used to say, 'That's a funny name for a girl!' Hardly anyone had heard of my dad's hero, Bobby Charlton. My big brothers are called Wembley, Striker, and Semi (we reached the semi finals that year); then it's Bobby, and last of all, me.

We were brought up on football right from the first whistle. Babies in our house didn't dribble drool: as soon as we could toddle we dribbled footballs! We never had soppy plastic rattles with baby bells: no, we went straight on to big, wooden football rattles. And when we were little, Mum hardly ever shouted at us: if we were naughty she just blew a whistle and produced a yellow card. Two yellow cards meant straight to bed – and NO arguing with the ref! Bobby and I were always getting sent off!

We're a kind of team, Bobby and I, so when he has a problem, it's my problem too.

Well, one Friday Bobby came in gasping: 'Queenie comin', Charlie – me's agiving f'owers – got no goalie kit!' The Queen was visiting Bobby's school, and he had been chosen to give her a bouquet; more than anything in the whole world, Bobby wanted to wear his team's goalie kit for the royal appointment!

'Mum . . .' I began. But I already knew what she was going to say – 'I'm sorry, Charlie, but we can't afford it. Perhaps when your father . . .'

Dad lost his job when the factory closed. He helps with the football at Bobby's school, but not for money. Bobby's face slipped and his eyes went all swimmy. I couldn't let him down.

'I'll get the money somehow,' I
told him. 'I'll work on it.'

Chapter 2

It wasn't until the school fête that I realised Bobby was working on it too.

Bobby was doing 'Beat the Goalie'. He's the best goalie in his class! I used to get jealous because his school has real goal posts, but we only have traffic cones. And he gets to go by taxi. You see, Bobby goes to a special school 'cos he's got Down's

syndrome. Mum says we're all
special. Just different.

Well, we were at the school
fête, and Bobby stood in the goal,
running on the spot. He jigged a

bit, then flung himself at the ball
– *whoosh*! – flat out. He never
worries about hurting himself: he
just goes for it – *woomph*!

In between goals he trotted
over to me, peered in the money
jar, and grinned. All afternoon he
shouted, ''Ow much? 'Ow much
now, Charlie?' But still I didn't
get it. Not till the very end of the
afternoon when he shook the
can and cried,

'Nuff for a goalie top,
Charlie?'
did the penny
drop:
Bobby thought
the money was for him!

'Nuff now?'

His eyes were all beamy bright. It was like in those cartoons when you seen pound signs in people's eyes. Well, I could see goalie kits in Bobby's. I stood there, shaking my head. And his eyes went all cloudy; his face crinkled up, not understanding.

'Goalie kit?' For a second the light in his face swooshed on again.

'No! The money's for the new swimming pool.'

'Goalie kit!' he wailed, and shot up the goal post, wrapping himself round the crossbar.

'I wan' my goalie kit!' he yelled.

All these people appeared.
'Ooh dear,' they clucked, 'poor
little lamb – he'll hurt himself!'

They were worried about
Bobby hurting himself. I was
worried about getting him down!
Help! What would Mum do?

I grabbed a lolly wrapper,
flashed it at Bobby, and yelled:
'Yellow card!' Bobby glared. I
glared back. The audience carried
on clucking.

'I'm going to count to five, and
then it'll be the red,' I tried.
'One, two . . .' Bobby clung on
tighter.

Then Dad sailed through the
crowd. Phew! He lifted his arms
up and said: 'Never argue with
the ref, Bobs!' Bobby dropped
into a big hug and Dad swung
him onto his shoulders, saying,
'Always accept the ref's decision,

and hold your head high!'

They galloped off to throw sponges at a teacher.

I thought it was all over. And I hoped Bobby would forget about the goalie kit. He often forgets which way round his tee shirt goes, or when it's his turn to do the washing up, but some things stick in his mind like chewing gum. This was one of them!

Chapter 3

Next morning Bobby and I went shopping. We passed Kevin Joggs from my class. He stuck his tongue out at me, and then pulled his eyes down all slitty and tried to catch Bobby's attention. I felt like kicking him you-know-where, but I could hear Dad's 'Hold your head high, and walk away'. So I grabbed Bobby's arm and shouted, 'Look, Bobby.

Come and see the one-man band!'

Brilliant save, I thought . . .

Bobby sat on the pavement cross-legged, and rocked happily. The music man drummed away. Bobby's fingers waggled on his knees in time to the music. He's got lovely, waggly fingers that all move at different times. I don't know anyone who's got fingers like Bobby's. Two white mice ran round the rim of the man's top hat, and Bobby's eyes went as round as circles as he watched. Then a new problem hit me: how was I going to get Bobby away from the busker? My brilliant save was turning into an own goal . . . I gave Bobby some pennies. He slipped them into his pocket and said, 'Goalie top!'

'No – put them in the hat!'

'Goalie?' he begged.

I bobbed beneath the white mice and whispered in the music man's ear. He winked at me, and galloped into, 'Oh when the saints . . .'

Then he tipped his hat to Bobby, saying: 'Here's to you, young 'un. I've got to be going now.'

'Me's goin' to see the Queen,' Bobby said proudly.

'Well don't chase any mice under her chair!' he replied, holding out a mouse for Bobby to stroke.

Chuckling, Bobby dropped the coins in the hat. But he did look at that hat in a very odd way . . .

It was quiet when we got back home. Dad had taken the big ones to an all day tournament, and Mum was helping Gran. I made sandwiches, listening to the babble of Bobby's 'Best Goals' video from the back room. He watches that video over and over. I'd just about finished when I realised something was wrong . . . badly wrong. The whole house had gone quiet. It was the sort of quiet you get while waiting for a penalty. That special sort of quiet which tells me Bobby's up to mischief or . . . in trouble. I ran from the kitchen. The front door was wide open. The street was empty. Should I go looking, or phone Mum? The police? I heard a siren, and felt sick.

Tearing down the street I scanned the side roads frantically. Traffic roared from the main road. What if he'd tried to cross? It was really fast – he wasn't allowed there by himself . . . I ran faster, gasping. How would I tell Mum? My feet pounded the pavement, my eyes stung. At the junction a massive lorry thundered by. Two boy racers screeched their brakes. Another siren wailed. I turned. My stomach somersaulted at the sight before me: a huge crowd gathered by the shops. They were grouped round something. An accident? Bobby! I tore up to them, smudging away tears with my jersey.

'Let me through!' I pulled wildly at the people. 'It's my brother, it's . . .'

The crowd parted, and there, on the pavement, was . . . 'Bobby?' I gulped.

He was wearing Mum's pink, wedding hat, the one with roses round the rim, dangling a tambourine, twiddling a football rattle, and banging an old Coke tin. Looking at me with his biggest crack-your-face-in-half grin, he said, ''Ello, Charlie!'

Everyone was smiling: great, stupid, happy smiles. And I just stood there with tears running down my cheeks.

Bobby belted out a mixture of

football songs, stringing together
all his favourite bits: 'Football's
comin' 'ome, it's comin' 'ome' –
a bit of humming and
tambourine crashing – 'Swing
low, sweet Charlie 'ot' and ending
up with: 'Oh whe' the sai'ts go
munching in . . .'

The crowd clapped, sang along and tossed coins into the bobble hat at Bobby's feet.

Well, Mum laughed till the tears ran down her face when I told her the story! Bobby did a repeat performance for the family, and loved every minute of it!

Chapter 4

But I felt pretty fed up as I set off for school the next day: the Queen's visit was getting nearer, and I was no closer to getting his kit. Even if I saved up all my pocket money I'd still only have enough for a pair of football socks!

'We're going to start a new project on letter writing,' Ms Stadia announced in literacy

hour. Boring or what?! I stared
out of the window.

'I want you all to write to
someone famous. We'll see if we
get any replies!'

That was the starting whistle!
Kick off! I couldn't write fast
enough: 'Dear Mr Brooks,' – I
had to write to Bobby's favourite
goalie! I told him how Bobby has
his pictures all round the house,
and how he runs around like an
aeroplane whenever he watches a
save, and all about the Queen
coming to his school, and the
busking expedition . . . Ms Stadia
said I was a bit short on full
stops, but she smiled. I think she
liked it. At the end I put: 'P.S. It's
Bobby's birthday on the 27th.

Mum says we shouldn't ask for things, but I know he'd be dead chuffed if you sent him a photograph.'

Well, other people started getting replies. But nothing came to our house.

Every morning I rushed downstairs to meet the postman, hoping and hoping. And every morning there'd be a little pile of brown bills. Never mind, he might still send a birthday card, I told myself. I could hardly sleep the night before Bobby's birthday, and in the morning I leapt down and sat on the doormat, waiting. The flap opened; cards plopped onto my lap. I flipped through them, really excited. But it wasn't there. No club crest. Nothing.

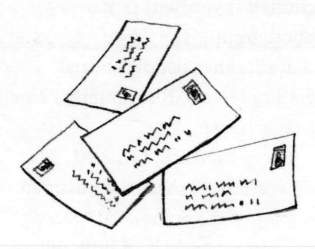

'Wadsamatter, Charlie?' Bobby asked when he saw me, and I tried to smile. I tried really hard to be cheerful, but Mum could see I was moping. She'd knitted him a jumper in club colours. It was really nice, and he liked it. But I was still disappointed.

'Cheer up,' Mum said, giving me a hug. 'There's still second post. Now why don't you go down to the rec while I decorate the birthday cake?'

I always feel better once I'm on a football pitch. Bobby went in goal. Jigging. I used to think that his jigging was magic, that it told him which way to dive.

Kevin Joggs pressed his face against the netting. 'Nice jumper,' he said sarcastically, 'yer mum knit it?'

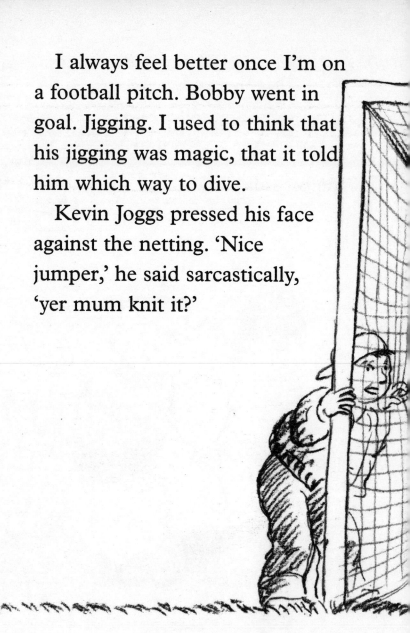

Bobby was too busy watching the ball to notice. I started to run up, and when I was just a metre away Kevin yelled: 'Girls are useless – they can't kick straight!'

I looked up for a second, and lost my rhythm. I was too close. I kicked with my left. And I knew as I watched the ball loop in slow motion where it would end.

'Post, post.' Kevin was jumping up and down. 'Girly whirly post!' he chanted. 'Told you girls can't play!'

Bobby swung round. 'Charlie's good!' he said angrily.

'Call that good?' Kevin sneered. 'A monkey could kick better than that!'

'Bobby, don't . . .' I called as he moved forward, clenching his hands. 'Please, Bobby, don't fight!'

Bobby walked right up to the netting.

He's going to hit him! I ran forward.

'You watch,' Bobby shouted. 'She gooder 'an you.'

He lifted his chin and turned away really calmly, collected the ball, and passed it to me. I was so proud.

'You show 'im, Charlie.'

I stepped back. Measured the run up. This one had to be good. I wanted it to power into the back of the net out the other side and right into Kevin's sneery smile. I trotted up slowly. Stay calm. Foot back. *Pow*!

'OK?' I said to Kevin, casual but pleased. 'See?'

'Mongrel,' he hissed, 'your brother's a mongrel . . .'

'He is NOT!' I growled. 'He's the best goalie in his school – now push off!'

He moved away, but then turned and smiled at Bobby, an awful, sickly smile.

He cooed, 'You are a mongrel, aren't you? Tell your silly sister you're a mongrel.'

'Charlie . . .' Bobby began, all desperate. He knew the smiling was nasty, but he couldn't understand it. His eyes were really hurting, begging.

I went bananas!

I hurled myself. Kevin didn't even see me coming. I floored him – flat on his fat belly. My fists hammered his back, hammering out that cooing voice.

'Stop, Charlie, stop,' Bobby tugged. Kevin grunted. I pushed his face into the mud.

'No fightin', Charlie – head high!'

I went limp. Bobby was right. I'd let Dad down. Staggering to my feet, I fought to hold back hot tears.

'Beat him a' football, Charlie,'
he nodded towards the goal.
'Football . . .'

'Challenge you to a shoot out!'
I said loudly and coldly. He
looked around. A clump of other
children had gathered.

'Go on,' said Jamie, 'she's only
a girl – even you could beat her.'

'Yeah, all right,' Kevin said.
'Yeah – I'll show her.'

He stuck his chest out, but there was a slight wobble in his walk. He ran up and walloped the ball into the top corner. A perfect penalty. He swaggered to the side.

'You go in goal,' he said to
Jamie. 'Her brother'd cheat!'

'Go, Charlton!' one of the girls
called. 'You can do it!'

I looked at the goal. The ball. I
ran forward, gaining speed, and
kicked. It was in! A cheer went
up.

The next couple went in. Two all. Level pegging. Kevin went for his third. Bobby knew which way it was coming. He dived brilliantly. His finger caught it, held it for a second. But it curled in. Bobby slunk off, and sat in a heap, hands over his head.

'Walk tall,' I whispered, as I lined up, feeling very small.

I hit hard and straight. But Jamie was there.

'Yees!' Jamie yelled. 'Three – two! You've lost!'

No one else cheered.

'It's best of five, anyway,' called Alison.

Kevin ran forward, full of confidence, and slammed the ball. It looked unstoppable. But then, somehow, Bobby was across the goal mouth, punching the ball away. A cheer rose from the sidelines.

My chance to equalise!

Worse than any of the other run ups. It had to go in . . . At the very last second I saw Jamie

move. In a snap moment I
changed foot, changed plan, and
watched the ball sail the opposite
way to the goalie. It crashed into
the post.

'Ohh . . .' went the group. It
bounced . . . and landed just
inside the line!

'Ahhh . . .' went the crowd.

I was back with a chance!

Everyone was still for the last round, except Bobby, who jigged a little more than usual. His face was crinkled up in concentration. There was just him and the ball. The ball flew. Bobby flew. Thud! He smashed it out!

Holding his arms out like an
aeroplane he circled the goal,
singing, ''Ere we go, 'ere we go,
football's comin' 'ome, it's
comin' . . .'

'You've done it, Charlie,' Rasheda shouted. But I hadn't done it. Not yet. This one had to go in. This shot was for all the girls in the world, and for Bobby not fighting . . .

I stood still for ages. A tall figure loped in our direction, but I shut him out. I shut out the ring of spectators, and even blotted out Bobby, who was watching through split fingers. There was just me and those posts. This time there could be no risks, no last minute changes . . . I ran, looked, kicked and . . . closed my eyes.

'Waddagoal! Waddagoal!'
Bobby's voice rang over the
cheers.

I sank to my knees, exhausted.
A huge shadow fell across me.
Mountainous. I stared up. The
mountain was jigging from foot
to foot, like Bobby does. And
grinning a little, jiggy smile, like
Bobby when he's nervous.

'Charlie?' Will Brooks' voice
was deep and warm. 'Your
mother said I'd find you here –
I've brought a birthday card for
Bobby . . .'

'Yees!' I shrieked, pulling my
elbows down and my fists up.
'Yees!!'

Before I could blurt out my
thanks, Bobby ran towards us. He
took one look at the smiling
mountain, and flung himself, all
arms and legs, around his
favourite goalie hero!

'Waddasave, waddasave!' he
yelled, and together they twirled
round the rec singing, 'Oh when
the sai'ts go munching in . . .'

It was brilliant!

Then Dad arrived and started
doing his vindaloo war dance.
Embarrassing or what? But even
that didn't spoil Bobby's big day.
Mum arrived with the cake, and

the older ones clutched
autograph books.

Bobby sat with his birthday
card. He gazed and gazed at the
team photo. He didn't even
notice the sports bag, until
someone prodded him and
pointed. Even then, he didn't
understand that it was for him!
His eyes were as wide as footballs
when he unzipped it and found –
a brand new goalie kit with
'BOBBY' in big letters on the
back.

He stared and stared . . .
Putting out one finger he touched
it, and pulled away quickly as if it
were hot. Then he put out
another finger and stroked it
gently, like a fragile creature.

All his fingers began to waggle
up and down in the silky fabric,
before he scooped it to him,
hugging and rocking and smiling.
It was the best birthday ever!

Chapter 5

And now, for the first time in my life, I'm sitting down to write a thank-you letter without Mum nagging me! At the top I've done a crest – like the ones you get on cereal packets. It says: 'Bobby: by appointment to H.M. the Queen.' Underneath I've drawn a picture of him all dressed up in his goalie kit. The Queen is beaming at him and holding his bunch of flowers.

The flowers are smiling. Bobby's smile is so big it's banging into his ears – almost booting his ears into the goal. Even the ball is grinning!

'Dear Mr' I begin; then I tippex out the Mr and write 'Dear Will'. We're on first name terms, now, Bobby's goalie mountain and me!

About the Author

Sophie Smiley was born in a Dominican monastery – she says she had a very happy childhood surrounded by Fra Angelicos and Ethopian priests! She now teaches English and is also a staff member of Forest School Camps, working with both the able and those with learning difficulties. She is married and has two children and they all live in Cambridge.

About the Illustrator

Michael Foreman is one of the most talented and popular creators of children's books today. He has won the Kate Greenaway Medal for illustration twice and his highly acclaimed books are published all over the world. He is married, has three sons and divides his time between St Ives in Cornwall and London.

Have you read the other
books about Bobby, Charlton,
and their football-mad family?

Team Trouble

Join Charlton and her football mad family
for another adventure . . . Semi has an
illness, the worst thing possible: he stops
talking and starts grunting, he has
something yucky on his back, and he
wears flowery shirts – eurgh! Worst of all,
he stops liking football! Can Charlton and
Bobby bring their brilliant bro back into
the team again . . .

Man of the Match

Bobby and Charlie are off to summer
camp. As soon as Bobby sees Paul, he
insists on being best friends with him,
even though Paul hides under his parka.
Of course Bobby insists on playing
football with Paul whatever the planned
activity really is. Charlie has her work cut
out to keep track of them – and she has a
big challenge of her own, too – a relay
race over water, and she's petrified!

SOPHIE SMILEY

TEAM TROUBLE

Illustrated by
MICHAEL FOREMAN

ISBN 9781842706848 £4.99

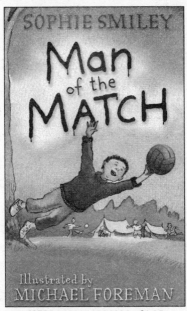

SOPHIE SMILEY

Man
of the
MATCH

Illustrated by
MICHAEL FOREMAN

ISBN 9781842704202 £4.99